STORY TIME
WITH THE
GREAT PAINTERS

STORY TIME
WITH THE
GREAT PAINTERS

compiled by Eric and Nancy Protter

THE
LION
PRESS

Publishers, New York

Credits

Camille Corot: Girl in Beret. Drawing, 290 x 222mm. Ca. 1831. Musée des Beaux-Arts, Lille.

Lucas Cranach the Elder: Portrait of a Man in Fur Hat. Brush drawing with water color. 23.8 x 16.7 cm. Ca. 1506. By Courtesy of the Trustees of the British Museum.

Honoré Daumier: Riot Scene. Pen and wash, 160 x 260 cm. Ca. 1845. Private collection.

Eugène Delacroix: Lion's Head. Water color, 178 x 191 mm. 1843. Cabinet des Dessins, Louvre, Paris.

Thomas Gainsborough: Landscape with Sheep and Two Shepherds. Water color, heightened with white, 215 x 280 mm. Clifford Duits, London.

Hiroshige, I: Landscape. Ink on paper, 27.9 x 16.9 cm. Late Edo Period. Courtesy of the Smithsonian Institute, Freer Gallery of Art, Washington D. C.

Kano Kuninobu Eitoku: Sennin Viewing Chokoro Riding his Magic Horse (part of triptych). Ink on paper. 25⅝ x 24½ inches. 16th century. Seattle Art Museum, Margaret E. Fuller purchase fund.

Oskar Kokoschka: View of Stockholm Harbor. Oil on canvas. Private collection.

Claude Monet: Nymphéas. Oil on canvas. 1904. Musée de Louvre, Paris.

Emil Nolde: Fish. Water color, 13½ x 18½ inches. Frederick B. Deknatel.

Harmenszoon van Rijn Rembrandt: An Elephant. Black chalk, 230 x 340 mm. 1637. Graphische Sammlung Albertina, Vienna.

J. M. W. Turner: Dazio Grande, water color. 9 x 10⅞ inches. Ca. 1841-45. Collection Richard Brown Baker.

Vincent van Gogh: The Enclosed Field. Oil on canvas, 28½ x 36¼ inches. 1890. Rijksmuseum Kröller-Müller, Otterlo, Holland.

Vincent van Gogh: View of Saintes Maries. Oil on canvas, 25¼ x 20¾ inches. 1888. Rijksmuseum Kröller-Müller, Otterlo, Holland.

A. van Ostade: Peasants Dancing. Pen and bistre wash, 163 x 208 mm. 1636. Teyler Museum, Haarlem.

Contents

Camille Corot: Girl in Beret.

The Fairy

Once upon a time there lived a widow with her two daughters. Because the older girl was her mother's favorite, she did nothing all day except sleep and dress in exquisite silken gowns. The younger girl, on the other hand, never enjoyed a moment's rest. She had to perform all the heavy chores of the household. She stoked the fire, swept and scrubbed the floors, and cleaned the house. Three times a day she fetched water from a well several hundred yards from the house. But the older sister was very jealous because her sister was exceptionally beautiful and good-natured in spite of her sad situation.

One day while the beautiful girl was filling her buckets at the well, she saw an old, wrinkled woman coming out of the woods. She approached the young girl and asked her for a drink of water.

The girl raised the heavy bucket to the old woman's mouth so that she could drink more easily.

"There," said the girl. "I hope the water has refreshed you. Is there anything else I can do for you?"

. . . She was exceptionally beautiful and good-natured in spite of her sad situation.

"No, thank you, my dear," the old woman replied in a soft voice. "You have been very kind to me. You will be rewarded when you reach home."

As the girl returned home, she saw her mother standing at the door, angrily waving a stick.

"What took you so long? Don't you know that your sister and I are thirsty? Have you no consideration for others?" she shouted meanacingly.

"I came back as fast as I could, Mother," the girl explained. "I am sorry to have kept you waiting. But at the well I met a frail old lady who needed some help."

As she spoke, an amazing thing happened. Every time she said a word, a magnificent gem—diamond, ruby, sapphire, emerald—fell from her hair.

Her mother immediately realized what had happened.

"You silly girl," she screamed. "That was no old lady you met at the well. She was a fairy. You are so stupid that you didn't even recognize her. You will see what will happen when I send your clever sister to the well."

The next day the older sister dressed in her finest clothes. She took the two empty buckets and slowly trudged to the well. After she had filled the first bucket with water, a lovely young woman appeared, dressed in a beautiful silk dress. The girl, who did not realize that this was the same fairy in disguise, was embarrassed to be seen filling buckets of water by a beautiful woman.

When the fairy asked her for a drink of water, the sister snapped: "Go fetch it yourself."

"You are not very nice nor are you very helpful," answered the fairy. "Nevertheless, you will receive your reward, too."

The older sister didn't even thank the fairy. She ran home as fast as she could, wondering what her gift would be.

"Now," said the mother to the younger daughter, "you will see what a smart person gets when she talks to the magic people."

But as soon as the elder sister spoke, snakes and worms fell to the ground.

This so infuriated the mother that she chased her younger daughter out of the house, blaming her for the older sister's dreadful fate.

The poor girl ran into the forest. When she had become tired out from running, she stopped to rest. She sat down on a rock and began to sob bitterly. Just at that time a prince was hunting near the rock and saw the beautiful girl. When he heard her sad weeping, he stopped his horse at her side and asked her what was wrong.

As the beautiful girl looked up at the prince, she fell silent. He reached out his hand and they both smiled. The prince helped her onto his horse and they rode away to his castle. They were married the next day, and for many, many years ruled over a happy kingdom.

A. van Ostade: Peasants Dancing.

*... for the inn was a jolly place and the local folk
were having a merry time singing and dancing ...*

Hudden and Dudden and Donald O'Neary

In Ireland long ago, there lived two prosperous farmers named Hudden and Dudden. Neither had a worry in the world. Each one owned hundreds of cattle and sheep, acres of fine farmland and some of the best fruit orchards in their part of the country. But despite this wealth the two farmers were unhappy. Between their farms was a small plot of land—not more than half an acre—that belonged to Donald O'Neary. Now, Donald was a good sort of man, and though he lived in a poor shack and owned only one cow, he was always cheerful. Why O'Neary irritated the two rich farmers so much nobody knew. But Hudden and Dudden lay awake many a night planning how to get rid of Donald.

Early one morning, Hudden ran to his neighbor's house and knocked on the door.

"Dudden," he exclaimed, "I have thought of a way to get rid of O'Neary!"

"Look," he continued, "if we kill his cow, Daisy, he'll starve to death. And rather than starve, he'll sell us his land."

Dudden thought this was an excellent idea, so they agreed to kill the cow that very night.

The next morning when Donald found Daisy dead, he was very upset. As he was doing his chores, he thought of a plan. He skinned the cow and placed its hide over his shoulder. Then he set out for the country fair. Before he got there, he made several slits in the hide, placed a coin in each slit and walked into the nearest inn. Carefully, he hung the hide on a coat hanger and sat down.

"Serve me the best food you've got!" he commanded the innkeeper. But he looked suspiciously at Donald's poor clothes and shook his head.

"Do you think I can't pay you?" asked Donald. "Well, stop worrying. Do you see that hide over there? It gives me all the money I need."

The innkeeper looked at Donald as if he were crazy. But he changed his mind when a coin dropped to the floor after Donald had slapped the hide with his stick.

"A most remarkable hide," said the innkeeper.

"That it is. That it is," replied Donald.

"And how much would you want for it? A golden coin?"

Donald laughed. "It's not for sale, innkeeper," he said sternly. "After all, it's kept me going for the last ten years." Donald whacked the hide again, and another coin popped out.

By this time the innkeeper was ready to give Donald all the money he had. After much discussion Donald accepted his offer, saying that it was only fair for someone else to benefit from the marvelous hide.

He finished his meal and left. On the way home he stopped at Hudden's house.

"Neighbor," he said, "would you lend me your money scale?"

Hudden couldn't imagine why Donald O'Neary would need a money scale, but he lent it to him anyway.

At home Donald pulled out all the gold he had received and weighed each piece. When he had finished, he returned the scale, not realizing that one of the coins had stuck to it.

Hudden was thunderstruck when he saw the gold. As soon as Donald left, he threw on his coat and ran to Dudden's house.

"What is the matter?" Dudden asked when he saw his friend standing at the door.

"It's O'Neary. He's made a fortune and he's just finished weighing all his gold."

"Now how can that be?" said Dudden. "We had better find out."

Thus Hudden and Dudden set out for O'Neary's shack. When they walked in, they let out a shout of surprise. Neatly stacked in rows of five pieces were piles of gold coins.

"O'Neary, where did you get the gold?" they asked.

"Well, since you're such nice people, I'll tell you," replied Donald. "This morning when I found old Daisy dead, I wondered how I could get some money for her. And do you know what I found out? For some reason or other, cowhides are worth their weight in gold."

Hudden and Dudden did not reply, nor did they say goodbye to Donald— they just rushed out the door.

They ran to their cowsheds and slaughtered all their cattle. The next morning they piled two carts with hides and set off to the fair. As they approached the tannery, they shouted: "Hides, hides! Does anyone here need hides?"

"How much do you want for them?" someone asked.

"Why their weight in gold!" Hudden and Dudden could not understand why everybody was laughing at them.

As they reached the market, they shouted: "Hides for sale! Hides for sale!"

And when they were asked how much they wanted for the hides, they repeated: "Their weight in gold."

But the innkeeper, who had been tricked by Donald the day before, was in the crowd. He rushed up to their carts, pulled them down and gave each one a thrashing, believing that Hudden and Dudden were part of a gang of bandits.

When they realized how neatly Donald had tricked them, they were even more angry with him than before.

They sneaked back to his shack and crept up behind him and threw him into a sack. They tied the sack and ran a pole through the knot. Each of the farmers lifted an end of the pole. Then they started toward the nearest lake to dump O'Neary into the water.

Thomas Gainsborough: Landscape with Sheep and Two Men.

...he met a friend.
   Together, they sat down on a fallen tree trunk
   and told each other fanciful tales...

But even the nearest lake was far away and the two farmers were tired out by now.

When they passed an inn, they decided to stop and rest.

"We'll be back soon enough, you wretch!" said Dudden to Donald O'Neary.

Donald didn't say a word but waited until he heard Hudden singing. That was what he had expected to happen. For the inn was a jolly place, and the local folk were having a merry time singing and dancing.

When Donald heard someone coming up the road he shouted: "I won't marry her! I refuse to marry her! I won't, I won't."

"And who won't you marry?" asked a shepherd who was driving his flock of sheep to market.

"The king's daughter!" replied Donald. "Twice, I've been lucky enough to escape. But this time, they've dumped me in this sack. I don't know how I'll manage to get away."

"The king's daughter," said the shepherd. He scratched his head. "Why I'd give anything to take your place."

"All right, then. Untie the sack and take my place."

"I won't have any more use for my sheep," said the shepherd, "you might as well take them."

Then he crawled into the sack. Donald had tied it so that it could easily be undone. For he meant the shepherd no harm.

Then he left, driving the flock of sheep home. But before he got there, he met a friend. Together they sat down on a fallen tree trunk and talked.

Soon Hudden and Dudden came out of the inn. They lifted the sack and continued on their way.

"I don't know how it's possible," said Dudden, "but it seems to me that Donald has put on some weight!"

"It doesn't make much difference," replied Hudden. "For we're almost there."

20

"Good, good!" shouted the shepherd happily.

"I'm glad you're pleased," said Dudden. "We are, too. Now you'll never bother us again."

And they pitched the sack into the lake. Without a moment's hesitation, they turned around and started home.

But when they neared their farms, they could not believe what they saw. There was Donald O'Neary surrounded by his new flock of sheep.

"How can that be?" they asked him. "Didn't we just dump you in the lake?"

"That you did," replied O'Neary. "But you couldn't have done me a greater favor. For at the bottom of the lake there are thousands of sheep. I just brought a few with me this time. Later on I shall go back for more."

"Donald," said Hudden, "surely you don't want them all for yourself. We'll always be good neighbors if you'll only show us where to find them."

"I really shouldn't," said Donald, "considering the trick you played on me."

"I'll tell you what," said Dudden. "If you show us where we can find the sheep, Hudden and I will each give you a few acres of land."

"All right! We'll let bygones be bygones!"

Thus the three set out for the lake. When they reached it, Donald told them to lean forward and to look carefully into the water. Then, as they were searching for the sheep, Donald gave them both a push, and with loud cries—they fell into the lake.

As they emerged from the water, they saw Donald standing at the edge of the lake.

"Well, friends, have you learned your lesson?" he asked.

Ashamed at their stupidity, they gravely nodded their heads.

Then the three neighbors went home together. From that day on, they were the best of friends. Their farms prospered and they lived together happily.

Hiroshige I: Landscape.

. . . The father had to make a trip,
far beyond the mountains
that rose majestically behind their tiny village . . .

The Mirror

In Japan many, many years ago, there lived a business man, his wife and their lovely daughter. She was as pretty as her mother and as wise as her father.

One day the father had to go to a large city far beyond the tall mountains that surrounded their tiny village. He was sad for he knew that he would not see his wife and daughter for many weeks. As he left, he tenderly kissed his wife and told her, "I shall return when the full moon reappears in the heavens. When I come back, I promise to bring you something very beautiful."

The young wife was worried as she watched her husband leave. Because she had never been farther away from home than the next village, she had thought that traveling in unknown parts of the country would be dangerous. Anxiously she awaited him. When the full moon finally rose in the heavens, she dressed herself and her daughter in their finest clothes.

And, as he had promised, the husband returned to their house. After they joyfully greeted each other, he carefully unpacked the present he had promised his wife.

"I have brought you a *tagami*—a mirror," he said. "Look into it carefully and tell me what you see!"

She carefully opened a delicately carved ivory box and saw a round silver disk. One side was decorated with colorfully painted flowers, animals, birds, and figures. The other side really surprised her, though. It was a gleaming, highly polished surface that reflected the face of a lovely young woman. But what astonished her was that every time her lips moved, the lips of the lady in the disk also moved. "And why should the lady wear the same dress that I wear?" she wondered.

The husband smiled when he saw his wife's puzzled face. He explained to her what a mirror was and that all the women in the large cities owned them.

The wife was very pleased with her gift. It was something new, something to be treasured. She thought it was such a remarkable object that she did not even show it to her neighbors. No one will ever know how many times she looked at herself.

One day she decided it was not good to look at oneself so much. So she put the mirror in its ivory box and stored it with her few other valuable possessions.

As the years passed, the couple's young daughter grew into a beautiful young woman. By the time she was twenty years old, she looked exactly like her mother had at that age. Worried that vanity might overcome her daughter if she were to realize her beauty, the mother kept the mirror a secret. Consequently, the girl grew up as innocently as her mother had, unaware of her great beauty.

In the spring the mother became very ill. Although her husband and daughter tried to nurse her, she became weaker and weaker. One day, she asked her daughter to get the carved ivory box. Taking the mirror out of it, she placed it on her bed.

"My dearest child," she said, "I am certain that both you and your father know that I shall soon be dead. I want you to promise me that after I die, you will look into this shiny reflection every morning and every evening. For you will see me there and know that I shall always protect you."

After the mother died, the girl kept her promise. Every morning and night she removed the mirror from its carved ivory box and looked at it for a few minutes. There she saw her own lovely face, but she believed it to be her mother's before she had been sick.

Every day the girl talked to the mirror, telling the image all that had happened during the day.

One day her father, who was not aware of his wife's request, asked his daughter what she was doing. The girl told him of the promise she had made to her mother.

The father was so moved by his child's sweetness and innocence that he couldn't tell her that the face in the mirror was really her own.

The Princess and the Pea

There once lived a prince who very much wanted to marry a princess. He had looked north and south and east and west, but nowhere could he find the perfect princess. There was always something wrong: one was too short, one was too tall. One was too blond, the other not blond enough. One year after he had returned from his search to his magnificent castle perched high on a mountain, he was very sad. For this time he was sure that he would never find the girl of his dreams.

Before he had been home for a week, there was a terrible storm. Bolts of lightning flashed through the sky and rain fell as if it had been poured from buckets.

Before he went to bed the prince heard a loud rap at the castle gate. He opened the door himself. Standing outside was the most beautiful girl he had ever seen. She was lovely even though her hair was drenched and her clothes soaked from the driving rain.

When the prince asked her who she was, he was greatly surprised to learn that she was a princess from a distant kingdom. She had gotten lost in the storm.

"We shall soon enough find out if she is really a princess," said the queen to her son.

She went into the bedroom where the princess was to sleep and ordered

Vincent van Gogh: View of Saintes Maries.

...He returned to his magnificent castle perched high on a mountain...

the servants to remove all the bedclothes. Then she placed a single pea on the mattress and commanded that twenty more mattresses be piled on the bed. Placed on top of the mattresses were four quilts containing the finest eiderdown.

The next morning during breakfast, the prince asked the princess if she had slept well.

"I spent an awful night," replied the princess. "I don't think I slept for more than five minutes. Something awfully hard was pressing into my back. In fact, this morning I noticed scratches and black and blue marks all over my back."

When the queen and her son heard the girl say this, they knew that she was truly a princess. For who else could feel a single pea through twenty mattresses and four quilts.

The prince was pleased. For he had found himself a lovely princess to help him rule the kingdom. In a few months a great wedding feast was held. And the prince and princess were married and lived happily ever after.

The Chestnut Thieves

There was a tiger who ruled over a sizeable area of land that contained many chestnut trees. Because the tiger was selfish, he warned all the other animals that they would die if he ever caught them stealing any chestnuts.

Though the tiger had plenty to eat, there were many animals living on his land who had a difficult time finding food. One day, the turtle visited her good friend the dog. After they had exchanged greetings and bemoaned the lack of good food, the turtle said:

"I wonder, my friend, if you have seen the tiger's chestnut trees? They are ripe now. Every time I pass them, my stomach growls."

"You are not the only one who feels that way," replied the dog. Then he looked around to make sure that he was not being overheard. "If you'd come with me, I'd take the chance and eat some of the delicious nuts."

"I had hoped you would say that," said the turtle. "I will gladly go with you. Why don't you come to my house tomorrow morning."

Early the next morning the dog arrived at the turtle's home. "Are you ready?" he asked.

Eugène Delacroix: Lion's Head.

... Within two minutes the lion was back,
his mane standing straight up
and his eyes rolling about
with an uncontrollable fear ...

"I am," said the turtle. She tucked a bag under her arm.

When they neared the chestnut trees, the turtle said, "There is one thing I must warn you about, my good friend. Occasionally, a chestnut will fall from the branches and land on you. This can hurt a great deal, but do not cry out. Just say the words *'choomp, choomp, choomp'* and the pain will stop."

"What do you take me for?" the dog answered in an insulted tone. "I know that if I were to bark, the tiger would hear me. Besides, I'm very brave. I can take quite a beating before letting out even the tiniest yelp."

"Well don't be insulted," said the turtle, trying to smoothe matters out. "I had to warn you. Because if the tiger notices us, you can run fast and get away. But I would be caught."

When the friends reached the chestnut trees, the turtle immediately set about gathering nuts. The dog was not content with what was lying on the ground. Noticing a huge clump of nuts hanging from a low branch, he jumped up and shook it vigorously. And sure enough, a large chestnut landed on the dog's nose.

"*Bow, wow, wow,*" wailed the dog. *Bow, wow, wow, wow, wow.*" Then, realizing what he had done, he ran away leaving the poor turtle stranded beneath a tree.

Within a minute, the tiger appeared. And the poor turtle had not been able to make her escape.

"So, turtle, you are the thief!" growled the tiger. "You know the punishment and now you will pay."

Swiftly the tiger placed the turtle in a clean white bag.

"Tiger," said the turtle. "You can see how dirty I am. Before I came here I wallowed in the mud near the river. Don't waste your nice clean bag. Why don't you use this old one, the one I brought, instead."

"That is very considerate of you," replied the tiger. And he placed the turtle in the old bag.

But there was another reason that the turtle had suggested this. She had noticed a small hole at the side of the old bag and she was sure that she could gnaw away at it, and escape.

And that is exactly what happened.

While the tiger was running back home, the turtle chewed the material until the hole was large enough for her to crawl out. And since the sack with the chestnuts was also inside the bag, the tiger did not realize that the weight he was carrying had indeed become lighter.

Thus while the tiger was rushing off in one direction, the turtle crept off toward the dog's home.

As soon as the tiger arrived at his cave, he ordered a large pot to be placed on the fire. "Tonight we will have the most delicious turtle soup," he said. Then he invited his friends to the feast.

When all were there, the tiger opened the bag and reached his paw in for the turtle. Furiously he searched inside the bag, shaking it and, finally, tearing it into shreds. But of course, the turtle was not there. Embarrassed at having been tricked in front of all his friends, the tiger roared with fury as his friends laughed. Then he lay down and sulked, hoping that the time would come when he would have his revenge.

In the meantime the dog apologized to the turtle, and swore that never again would he behave in such a cowardly fashion.

"Even if a chestnut were to hit me in the eye, I wouldn't whimper," he said. "And, if necessary, I would just say *'choomp, choomp, choomp'* so that the pain would go away."

"If you really mean what you say, I could be persuaded to give it another try," said the turtle.

"I mean it, my friend, I really mean it," said the dog.

"All right then. Let's set out tomorrow morning."

The next morning the two friends started on their way again. There were many chestnuts lying on the ground and soon their bag began to fill up. But suddenly a gust of wind sprang up and many chestnuts rained from the trees. One hit the dog squarely in the eye.

"Bow, wow, wow, wow" he barked and ran off in the direction of home, once again leaving the poor turtle behind. It seemed that this was what the tiger was waiting for because he was at the tree before you could count to ten. Without saying a word, he plopped the turtle into his bag and rushed home.

The dog, quite ashamed at deserting his friend, turned around just in time to see her being carried off by the huge beast.

He had to try to save his friend. He went to see the owl for advice. The owl brought out nutshells and seashells, broken glass, bells, scrap metal and a number of odds and ends that jingled and clattered. He tied all these articles together and hung them over the dog's body. Then he took an old pot and tied it on the dog's head. Dressed in this way, the dog didn't look like any creature that had ever been seen in the jungle.

"What you must do now," said the owl, "is to go to the river and hide. When the tiger comes down to the bank, jump around as wildly as you can. He will be frightened by the noise and even more scared when he sees you because he will think of you as a monster guarding the river."

In the meantime, the tiger had arrived home with the turtle. He took her out of the bag, but kept continuous watch over her. Then he again invited all his friends, including the elephant and the lion, to dinner. After they all had gathered in his cave, he started an enormous fire and asked his sons to go to the river to fetch some water. Within minutes the young tigers were back in the cave shaking and whimpering with fright.

"What is the matter?" everybody asked.

"A river monster is guarding the stream," they said. "And it is the most horrible thing we have ever encountered."

"Don't be ridiculous," exclaimed the tiger. "There is no such thing. But if you are such cowards, I'm sure one of our friends will fetch the water."

Instantly two hyenas volunteered. But within minutes they too returned shaking and howling.

"The cubs are right," they said. "There is a monster guarding the stream— a horrible thing the likes of which has never been seen before."

"I think you are all ridiculous," said the lion. "I agree with my friend the tiger that there is no such thing as a river monster. And though fetching water is

Harmenszoon van Rijn Rembrandt: An Elephant.

...The elephant lumbered off toward the river...

a task that is quite beneath me, I shall go to the river just to show you how silly you are."

But within two minutes the lion was back, his mane standing straight up and his eyes rolling about with uncontrollable fear.

"My friends," he finally managed to blurt out, "this is an evil day indeed. This beast, this horror that is standing at the river, looks most frightening. He also makes the most wicked gestures and noises that I have ever seen or heard. I was so frightened I had to lie down. But then when it came charging at me, I somehow managed to run away. I assure you, I just barely escaped with my life."

"How big is it?" asked the elephant.

"About the size of a leopard," replied the tiger cubs.

"Not at all," said the hyenas, "it is more the size of the lion."

"You could not be more wrong," said the lion. "It is at least as big as a zebra."

"Well, if it isn't as large as I am," said the elephant proudly, "I doubt very much that it can scare me."

Saying that, he lumbered off toward the river.

The dog, who was immensely pleased with the success he had in scaring all these dangerous animals, saw the elephant from far away.

"Courage," he said to himself, "have courage. Though the elephant is much larger, he is by no means more clever then the other animals."

As soon as the elephant approached the river bank, the dog left his hiding place, howling and growling and shaking his body so fast that he made even more terrible noises than he had with the other animals.

The elephant was completely surprised and he was so frightened that he did not even take a careful look at the dog. He let loose a tremendous trumpet blast, turned around, and ran back as fast as he could, his mighty feet making great footprints in the soft ground. As he came crashing into the cave, all the animals sensed that something supernatural must be at the river.

"It is unbelievable," the elephant gasped. "There must be a curse on us."

The tiger was bristling with anger. He sensed that once again he was to be deprived of his turtle soup. Therefore, he decided to go to the river himself. But feeling that it would be considerably safer if he were accompanied by the other animals, he called for silence.

"My good friends," he said, "clearly something peculiar is at the river's edge. However, I believe that if we all go down together we can outwit this monster. Certainly, we all have need of water and we can not permit ourselves to be deprived of it."

Though all the animals who had already confronted the strange beast were most hesistant in going down a second time, they did finally agree. And, in all the excitement they forgot about the turtle.

No sooner had all the animals left the cave when the turtle also departed. But she took a different route.

When the dog saw all the animals walking toward the river, he knew that he would not be able to frighten all of them at the same time. So he ran into the woods toward the turtle's home. He did not have to wait long for the turtle to appear.

Joyfully the two friends greeted each other. The turtle was not too surprised when the dog told his story. She had suspected that he would think of some scheme to try and rescue her. But before the dog went home that evening, he and the turtle agreed that no matter how hungry or tempted they might be, they would never again steal the tiger's chestnuts.

In the meantime, the tiger cubs, the hyenas, and the elephant were astonished to find absolutely no trace of the dreadful monster. The tiger who had been suspicious all along did not hide his contempt and teased his 'brave, brave' friends.

But he did not laugh when he returned home and discovered that his precious, big turtle had escaped the soup once again.

Tale of the Oki Islands

In the early fourteenth century, the Emperor Hojo Takatoki was the undisputed master of Japan. Because he wielded enormous power, no one dared oppose him. But one day, Oribe Shima—a samurai who resided at the Emperor's court—said something that so angered the Emperor Hojo, that Oribe was banished from the country. He was exiled to a miserable group of islands called the Oki Islands. There, each day, Oribe went for long walks along deserted paths that were straddled by beautiful trees.

It was very sad for one man to be exiled all alone. For Oribe it was unbearable because his beautiful young daughter Tokoyo was not allowed to go with him. After several years brave Tokoyo felt so miserable at being separated from her father that she decided to try to reach him. She was an excellent swimmer. As a child she used to dive with the women for pearls, deep beneath the sea.

Kano Kuninobu Eitoku: Sennin Viewing Chokoro Riding his Magic Horse.

After traveling for many days she reached the little fishing village of Akasaki, from where the Oki Islands could be seen on especially clear days. She talked to many fishermen and begged them to take her across the channel to the islands. But all refused because the Emperor had given strict orders that no one was to ever set foot there.

One day she decided to make the trip by herself. In the evening, after the sun had set, she went to the harbor and rented a small sailboat. She set out for the islands.

Although the sea was stormy, she managed to stay on course. Finally, late the next day, exhausted and hungry, she landed on the rocky shores of one of the islands. She moored the boat and climbed the cliffs til she reached a plateau. There she lay down and rested for a few hours. In the afternoon, she set out to find her father. Soon she met an old man and his attendant.

After having told him her story, she asked whether he knew where her father was.

"Indeed not," he replied "and let me give you some advice. People here will not answer your question even if they know where your father is. Every one is terribly afraid of the Emperor's wrath."

For the next few days, Tokoyo wandered all over the islands hoping to hear some word about her father. But she was afraid to ask any direct questions. Soon she ran out of money and had to beg for food.

One evening after she had prayed to Buddha in a small shrine, she heard a young girl sobbing bitterly. She looked around, and in the bright moonlight she saw a lovely young girl standing at the edge of a cliff. Beside her stood a priest, clapping his hands and reciting a prayer.

She ran over to the strange couple and arrived at the very instant when the priest was about to push the girl over the cliff into the roaring ocean below.

"What are you doing?" she asked while grasping the young girl's arm.

The priest looked at her sternly.

"I can see that you are not familiar with the customs of this island. I assure you that this is the saddest ceremony I have to perform each year. But indeed it must be done."

"What has to be done?" asked Tokoyo. "And why?"

"My dear child," replied the priest, "this island is cursed by an evil god called Yofune–Nushi. Each year we must sacrifice one young girl to him. Otherwise he will create great hurricanes and cause the death of many of our fishermen."

Tokoyo listened attentively. Then she spoke.

"Let me take her place. I have come here to find my father, Oribe Shima, a noble samurai. I have searched for him everywhere and yet I can not find him. I am so unhappy that I no longer care to live. Let me be the sacrifice."

She then took the white robe from the girl and put it on. Next she prayed that she might have enough courage to kill the evil god, Yofune–Nushi, if she got the opportunity. Then, as she approached the edge of the cliff, she pulled a magnificent dagger from its sheath, placed it between her teeth and dove into the roaring ocean. The priest and the girl looked into the ocean with great awe. They felt as if they had just witnessed a great miracle.

Tokoyo swam down through the clear water which glittered in the moonlight. Near the bottom she saw a huge cave carved out of rock and decorated with glistening shells. When she looked into the cave, she thought she saw a man seated on a throne of rock and pearly shells. As she entered the cave, with the dagger in her hand, for she thought that the man must be the evil god, she realized that it was only a wooden statue of the Emperor, Hojo Takatoki. Anger overwhelmed her at seeing his unwelcome figure. She was ready to slash at it when she realized that it would be better to bring the statue to the surface of the water. She undid her sash and fastened the statue to her.

As she started upward, a dragonlike creature covered from head to feet with scales swam in front of her. His eyes shone with hate and Tokoyo realized that he must be the evil god, Yofune–Nushi. Though she was frightened, she swam toward him. With all her power she plunged the dagger into the evil creature's eye. Completely surprised that a mortal would dare to fight him, the monster tried to find his way into the cave. But because he was half-blind, he could not find the entrance. Realizing that Yofune was momentarily dazed and confused, Tokoyo swam up to him and plunged the dagger through his heart. The evil god floundered about and with a great shudder—he died.

The priest and the girl who were still gazing into the water were astonished when they saw Tokoyo swim to the surface. But they were even more surprised when they saw the body of the dead sea monster float into view.

They ran down the cliff to help the exhausted Tokoyo.

All the island people gathered in the town. When Tokoyo arrived she was celebrated as a great heroine. For she had rid the island forever of its terrible curse.

News of the extraordinary event on the Oki Islands soon reached the Emperor. He had been sick for some time. He recovered miraculously when Tokoyo had brought his statue out of the cave. The Emperor realized that his illness had been due to a curse placed on him. Now that Tokoyo had recovered the statue, the curse was lifted.

He immediately ordered the release of Oribe Shima. After a few days of feasting and celebration, the samurai and his courageous daughter returned to the Emperor's palace. There they lived victoriously with dignity and in happiness.

Tokoyo gained lasting fame. Her deeds are still celebrated not only in the Oki Islands, but throughout all Japan.

The Turnip

As many years ago as there are stars in the sky, there once lived two brothers who had loyally served their king as soldiers. When it was time for them to be discharged from the service, it turned out that one of the brothers was quite poor, while the other brother had managed to become very wealthy.

The poor brother, trying his best to better himself, became a peasant. He worked diligently from early morning until late at night, but regardless of his efforts, success was not to be his. For years he could do no better than scrape the most meager living from the soil.

One day early in the summer, he noticed that one of the turnips he had planted that spring was growing to a fantastic size. It seemed that the vegetable would never cease growing and by midsummer it was so huge that it barely fitted onto his cart. He decided that because the turnip was truly unusual he would make a present of it to the king.

After much work, he and a friend managed to load it onto the cart. Because it was extraordinarily heavy, he did not use one or two oxen to pull the vehicle, but a team of four. And even these strong beasts had a hard time pulling it to the king's castle which was a few miles away.

"What an unusual thing," said the king when he viewed the gigantic turnip. "In my entire life I have never seen anything like it."

"My lord," replied the peasant, "I thought it would please you to know that such a magnificent turnip has grown on land owned by you. Therefore, I thought I should give it to you."

The king was greatly pleased by the peasant's kind thoughts, and he rewarded him amply. In fact, he bestowed such riches on him that the poor peasant was now every bit as wealthy—if not actually wealthier—than his brother.

When the rich brother heard of his brother's good fortune he was very annoyed. He was very envious of him and he stayed up late at night wondering what he might do to obtain the king's favors.

At last he decided that he would present the king with a sack of gold and a pair of Arabian horses. *"If the king has given my brother money, land, and cattle for a miserable turnip what will he not give to me when he sees my gifts?"*

When the king received the presents he asked:

"And why my good man are you bringing me these presents?"

"To please your majesty," lied the older brother, "it is but a token of my great esteem."

But the king was not to be deceived. He realized that the man standing before him was none other than the rich brother of the poor peasant who had brought him the turnip. He also realized that this man was unquestionably very greedy and that he expected great rewards. Therefore, he said:

"Presents such as yours deserve the greatest and rarest rewards. Come into the courtyard with me. My gift to you is of such size that you cannot possibly carry it away. Rather, you will have to cart it away."

When the rich brother heard this he was overjoyed for he imagined that he would be given a wagonful of precious jewels, gold, and other valuable trinkets.

The brother walked with the king into the courtyard and the expression on his face was one of great despair when he saw that his gift was nothing else but the huge turnip that his brother had brought the king earlier that month.

"Well," said the king with a wry smile on his face "how do you like your gift?" And then he continued with anger in his voice. "You are very lucky that I will not take your entire fortune as punishment for your greed. I never want to see you in my court again."

The rich brother walked home in great shame. Though it had been a costly lesson, he had learned that his greed could never serve anyone well. And, in time, he became a better person.

The Legend of Knockmany

One day, Finn McCool and his men were working on a bridge between Ireland and Scotland. Having worked for a few weeks on this project, Finn felt lonely for his wife, Oonagh, and took it into his head to go home and visit her. With Herculean strength he pulled a medium size fir tree from the ground, tore off its roots and branches, made a walking stick of it and set out on his way. Since Finn was a giant, each of his steps was equal to a hundred ordinary ones. So it did not take him long to reach his home, which was built on the very top of Knockmany Hill—one of the windiest spots in all Ireland.

Though it seemed strange to most people to build a house on this barren and miserably cold place, Finn had a good reason for living there. Another giant named Cuchulain had sworn to kill the great Finn McCool. And though Finn had fantastic strength, Cuchulain was even stronger. When he was angry, he could stamp his feet so hard that all the country around him shook. With one chop of his hand he could knock down ten trees. And since he had beaten all the giants of Ireland except Finn McCool—he swore that he would never rest until he had beaten Finn.

Although Finn never admitted his fear of Cuchulain to any of his friends, he lived in constant terror. And so he built his house on top of windy Knockmany Hill so that he could see the giant coming toward the place.

"God bless you, Oonagh," said Finn when he reached the door of his house.

"Welcome home, Finn," replied his wife.

After a few days at home Finn began to act nervous. After much coaxing, Oonagh at last got Finn to tell her what the matter was.

"I have a feeling that Cuchulain is looking for me at this very moment." He walked over to the window and looked at the country below. Then his entire body began to shake with fear.

"I see him below Dungannon, dear wife; he'll be here by noon tomorrow."

"And what am I to do?" he continued. "If I run away, I shall be disgraced. And if I stay here, he will break every bone in my body."

"Don't concern yourself," said Oonagh calmly. "Rely on me. I shall figure some way out of this mess."

She then went outside and built a huge fire. When black billows of smoke rose into the sky, she gave three shrill whistles. This was a signal that told strangers they were welcome to stop at the house for food and lodging.

In the meantime, Finn was upset. He paced up and down the length of his kitchen. Though Oonagh had gotten him out of many scrapes, he could not understand why she went out of her way to invite Cuchulain to their house.

"Oonagh," he said at last, "do you have a plan or am I to be disgraced?"

"Relax, my husband," replied Oonagh. "There's little to worry about. I know exactly what I am going to do. When the time comes, all that you'll have to do is follow my instructions."

As reassuring as these words were, Finn was still worried. He put his thumb in his mouth. Finn's thumb was a curious thing, for it gave him the ability to look into the future. Cuchulain also possessed a magic finger—the third finger on his right hand. If he were to lose that finger, his strength would be no greater than that of an ordinary man.

The next day at about midday, Cuchulain approached the mountain. Oonagh brought a cradle from the other room and made Finn lie down in it. Then she covered him up.

"Act as if you're a four-year-old child," Oonagh commanded.

Soon there was a loud rap and Oonagh went to the door to open it.

"Is this Finn McCool's house?" boomed a voice.

"That it is, good man," replied Oonagh. "Won't you come in?"

"Thank you kindly," said Cuchulain. "I suppose you are Mrs. McCool?"

"I am," Oonagh said, "and I'm sure that's nothing to be ashamed of."

"Indeed not," replied Cuchulain. "He has the reputation of being the strongest man in all Ireland. Is he at home?"

"No, he isn't," answered Oonagh. "He charged out of here yesterday, full of fury and anger. It seems that a giant called Cuchulain was looking for him at Dungannon. I hope for Cuchulain's sake that Finn doesn't find him. For if he does, Finn will beat him to a pulp."

"I wouldn't be so sure of that," said the giant, who had been listening attentively. "For I am Cuchulain. I've been looking for your husband for many years. I am ready at any time to dispute his claim of strength."

When Oonagh heard this, she glanced at Cuchulain with pity and disdain.

"Have you ever seen Finn?" she asked.

"How could I have?" replied Cuchulain. "As I've told you, he has avoided me for years."

"Well for your sake, I hope you'll never meet him. I think his size alone would frighten you to death. But in the meantime, Cuchulain, have you noticed how the wind is blowing through the door. Since Finn is not at home, I wonder if you'd oblige me by turning the house around. That's what Finn does when the wind is strong."

When Cuchulain heard this, he was surprised. He hadn't imagined that Finn would be that strong. He arose from the chair and pulled the middle finger of his right hand three times. Now he had extraordinary power and strength. He went outside and turned the house around. Finn, lying quietly in the cradle, was terrified when he felt the house move, but Oonagh betrayed no signs of fear.

As soon as Cuchulain returned she said, "I wonder if you'd do me another favor, since Finn is not here. We are badly in need of some water. Finn tells me that there is a well somewhere under the rocks below. If he hadn't gone looking for you, he would have pulled the rocks apart. I'd be most grateful if you could do that for me."

She led Cuchulain to a massive rock a few hundred yards away from the house. On each side jagged cliffs rose high into the sky. Before him a towering mountain range was partially hidden by low-lying clouds. After looking at the rock for some time, Cuchulain pulled the middle finger of his right hand twelve times. Then he bent over and tore an enormous cleft in the rock.

"Thank you so much," said Oonagh. "I am sure you must be hungry after all this work. Come into the house and let me fix you some food. Even though you and Finn are sworn enemies, he would not like it if I didn't show you hospitality in his house."

She placed before him four enormous hot cakes, which were stuffed with bacon, cabbage and solid-iron griddles. This food looked so delicious and smelled so good that Cuchulain, who was very hungry by this time, reached for one and took a huge bite. But no sooner had he done so when he let out a powerful yell. "Thunder and lightning! What kind of cake is this? Look, here are two of my teeth knocked out!"

"What is the matter?" Oonagh asked.

"Look, woman," Cuchulain shouted. "Two of my best teeth have been knocked out by this cake."

"I don't understand it," she replied. "This is what Finn eats every night. He

. . . On each side jagged cliffs rose high into the sky.
Before him a towering mountain range
was partially hidden by low-lying clouds . . .

J. M. W. Turner: Dazio Grande.

did tell me one evening that only he and his child in the cradle over there can eat these cakes. But I thought that anyone who thinks he can fight Finn can also manage his food. Well, here's another cake. Maybe this one won't be as hard."

Cuchulain picked it up and bit into it hard. Instantly there was another yell at least twice as loud as the first one. "Fury!" he shouted. "Take your cakes away, or I won't have a tooth left in my head. Here are two more gone."

"Well, my good man," Oonagh replied very coolly. "If you can't eat Finn's food, just say so quietly. Please don't wake the child over there. Though it seems that you have done it already."

Finn cried so loudly that Cuchulain was amazed to hear such noise coming from a child.

"Mother," shouted Finn. "I'm hungry. Please give me some food."

Oonagh walked to the cradle and placed a cake without an iron griddle in Finn's hand. He took it and happily munched away. When Cuchulain saw the little child eat food that had cost him four of his strongest teeth, he realized how fortunate he was not to have met Finn.

"I would have had no chance with the father, if his little son is capable of eating such food," he said to himself.

"I should like to take a look at the lad, Mrs. McCool," said Cuchulain.

"By all means," replied Oonagh. And turning to Finn she said, "show our guest something that will make your father proud of you."

Finn, who was dressed like a little boy, got up from the cradle and walked over to Cuchulain.

"Are you strong?" he asked in a deep voice.

"What a powerful voice you have for so small a child," Cuchulain exclaimed in wonderment.

"Can you squeeze water out of this white stone?" asked Finn, placing one into Cuchulain's hand, who tried without success.

"Well then give it to me, you poor, weak giant," said Finn.

He took the stone, and while Oonagh distracted Cuchulain for an instant, Finn exchanged the stone for curds. He squeezed until water oozed from his hand.

"I think I'll take a nap now," said Finn. "But let me warn you to go, before Father returns. Unless you want to be made into mincemeat."

By this time Cuchulain was convinced. He arose, shaking with fear, and told Oonagh that he would never return to this part of the country.

"There is only one thing that really fascinates me," Cuchulain said. "Before I leave, I wonder if you'd let me feel the kind of teeth Finn's lad has?"

"Go right ahead," said Oonagh. "Only remember, they're placed far back in his head, so you must put your fingers a good way in, if you want to feel them."

Cuchulain was amazed to find that such a young lad could have such a strong set of teeth. Then he let out a loud yell, for Finn had bitten off the middle finger of his right hand—the magic finger upon which his whole strength depended.

Now that Finn had his bitter enemy entirely at his mercy, he told him to leave and never return. The giant ran out the door as fast as he could, grateful that he had escaped with his life.

Lucas Cranach the Elder: Portrait of a Man in Fur Hat.

The Wishing Ring

In Germany many years ago, there once lived a farmer who worked his fields most conscientiously and still was unable to earn a living. No matter what he tried, luck seemed to work against him One year when the fields were ripe with wheat and it seemed that he would have a good harvest at last, a terrible storm arose and flooded his fields. Another year a late spring frost destroyed most of his fruits and vegetables. So it was not surprising that most of the time the farmer was in a bad mood. He complained bitterly about many things.

One fall afternoon while he was plowing his field, and moaning about his luck, an old witch appeared at his side.

"Farmer," she said, "why work so hard when it doesn't amount to anything?"

"What else can I do?" replied the farmer.

"Why there are lots of things you can do," she said. She pointed toward the setting sun and continued. "If you walk in a straight line in that direction for three days, you will come upon a cypress tree taller than all the others. If you want to become a rich man, all you have to do is to chop down that tree."

. . . the farmer grew enormously rich and the wish was still not wished . . .

Before Farmer John had a chance to ask any questions, the witch had disappeared.

Realizing that he had nothing to lose by following her advice, he took his axe and walked in the direction of the setting sun. And after three exhausting days of travel, found the cypress tree rising majestically beyond a cornfield. He began to chop it down and just before the tree fell, a bird's nest with two eggs came crashing to the ground. As the eggshells cracked open, an angry cloud appeared in the sky and lightning struck. A tiny eagle edged its way out of one egg. As the farmer watched, the eagle grew before his eyes. Soon he was as large as Farmer John. He flapped his wings and as he soared into the sky, he shouted back, "Thank you for having freed me, farmer. As a reward, I shall give you the little ring in the other egg. Even though it may look worthless, take good care of it because it is a magic ring. It will grant you one wish. But once you have wished, the ring will lose its magic power."

When the eagle had disappeared, the farmer looked at the other shell. It had cracked open, and sure enough, a most ordinary looking ring was lying inside it. He placed it on his finger and started on the long journey home.

When he reached the neighboring town, he decided to go to the jeweler and ask him to evaluate the ring. The goldsmith looked at it very carefully through his large magnifying glass and then shook his head.

"Completely worthless," he said. "It is an ordinary copper band."

"It's true that it's made from copper," replied Farmer John. "But you couldn't be more wrong about its worth. This is one of those extremely rare wishing rings. It can provide me with riches you haven't even thought about."

The jeweler was very impressed by what the farmer had just said. But he did not say anything. Instead, he made plans to steal the ring. He invited the farmer to his home to have dinner with him.

Quickly the jeweler put a sleeping potion into the wine and offered some to the farmer. Since he was terribly tired to begin with—having traveled for six days—the drug took effect immediately. Within minutes the farmer was sound asleep in his chair. The goldsmith slipped the magic ring from Farmer John's finger and replaced it with one that looked exactly like it. When the farmer awoke a few hours later, he apologized for having fallen asleep. Then he continued on his way without realizing that he had been cheated.

No sooner had the farmer left when the goldsmith overcome by greed, ran into his basement. He could think of nothing but filling the entire chamber with gold coins. He rubbed his hands, smiled, and then turned the magic ring. "I want this entire basement filled with gold coins," he whispered.

Gold coins rained from every part of the basement. Soon the jeweler was engulfed by the golden coins. His expression of joy sooned turned to one of horror when he realized that he could not move, that he was hopelessly trapped. "Stop," he shouted, "I have enough gold." But the gold did not stop falling. Not until every inch of the room, from floor to ceiling, was filled with the precious metal—burying the greedy jeweler in his fortune.

When the farmer arrived home he showed the ring to his wife and told her of its magic power.

"We don't own enough land, dear husband," she replied. "If we could just have a few more acres, I am sure that we could earn a decent living."

"No, my dear wife," John answered. "We must think very carefully before we make our wish. After all, if I work hard and if I have any luck, I'll be able to purchase more land. It would be a mistake to use our wish for that."

And the next year the farmer worked as hard as he had always worked. But for some reason he had no bad luck. For the first time in his life his harvest was excellent. With his profits he bought more land.

His wife then suggested that he wish for a better farmhouse and for more cattle. But again the farmer replied that with hard work and with the new land he would be able to buy those things the next year without having to use their wish.

One year followed the next and the wish had still not been wished. And each year the farmer worked harder than he ever had, and each year brought him more riches.

Twenty-five years after the farmer had come into possession of the ring, his wife said to him one day: "My dear husband, isn't it time for you to stop working so hard? The ring could bring you unimaginable wealth. You could be emperor, if you so chose! But instead, you still go into the field each day and you work."

"Life is long," replied the farmer "and who knows what might still happen. No, we must save the wish for the day when we really need it."

Thus the farmer grew enormously prosperous and the wish was still not wished.

Then one day, some fifty years after the farmer had obtained the ring, he and his wife died. And they were buried with their magic ring—which actually wasn't a magic ring at all. Yet somehow it made all their wishes come true.

The Imprisoned Water Princess

Once upon a time there lived two boys who were the best of friends. One was the son of a mighty maharajah and the other the son of a general. When the boys came of age, they decided to leave their kingdom and travel to other parts of the world. Thus, one day they said goodbye to their parents, mounted their horses and rode away. After having ridden for many days, they reached a forest so dense that the sun could hardly penetrate it. But before the sun had set, they came to a huge tree located next to a beautiful pond. They climbed onto one of the upper branches of the tree, believing that it would be safer than resting on the ground. From their perch they saw that the pond was crowded with brilliantly colored water lilies and multicolored ferns. As soon as the moon arose, the pond reflected its light, making it eerie and magical. As the night wore on, the two friends heard strange noises and saw strange shapes and shadows moving around in the woods.

Near midnight they heard a terrible roar. There was a great splashing in the pond as the water parted and a serpent rose to the surface. On its forehead was a diamond the size of an ostrich egg. The diamond glittered and sparkled and lit up the woods and pond nearby. The two friends knew at once that this must be the horrible sea monster that they had heard about when they were children. The diamond was worth more than all the money in the King's treasury. They watched in fear as the serpent swam ashore and removed the gem from his forehead. Then they listened as the creature slithered into the woods looking for food. At the same time it was hissing and roaring with anger.

When the monster had been in the forest for some time, and the two lads could no longer hear him, the general's son lowered himself to the ground. He walked over to the diamond and covered his eyes for its glare would have blinded him. When he reached the jewel he covered it with mud. Then he climbed back onto the tree.

As soon as the sea monster realized that the light had grown dim, he tried to rush back to the pond, hoping to find the jewel. But without the brilliant light he was hopelessly lost in the forest. And since he could not live on land for more than an hour at a time, he became weaker and weaker. In the distance, the two lads heard him shudder and shriek. At last they heard a most horrible groan and they knew that the creature had died.

They climbed down from the tree and dug up the jewel. Despite the mud that was sticking to it, the diamond sparkled brilliantly and illuminated the water. The two young men looked into the pond. To their great surprise they saw a magnificent palace on the bottom of the pond.

They dove into the water carrying the jewel with them. Passing through the palace gates they saw magnificent formal gardens with flowers they had never seen. But if the gardens were glorious, the palace itself was even more dazzling. It was built of solid gold. Its turrets were decorated with diamonds, rubies, sapphires, and emeralds. Strangely enough the castle seemed to be completely deserted. They wandered down long corridors and entered room after room. Nowhere was there a sign of life.

The two friends were about to leave, when they noticed a door that seemed to be woven of silver and gold threads. Entering, they found a lovely princess lying on a golden sofa.

"What are you doing here?" she asked completely surprised. "You must leave at once because the mighty sea monster who lives here will kill you if he finds you."

The two boys then explained how they had fooled the evil creature. To prove their story they showed the princess the enormous jewel they had brought with them. The princess was overjoyed to learn that she had been freed from her terrible life, and she asked the two boys to remain at the palace.

Soon the maharaja's son fell in love with her, and they were married. Time passed quickly for the three young people, until one day the maharaja's son decided to return to his own country.

He asked his friend to go home first to explain all that had taken place. Then, in a year he would return to the pond with servants and horses so that he and his wife could make a triumphant entrance home. The general's son agreed. He left his friend and the princess.

But things did not work out as they had planned. After the general's son had been gone for a month, the princess, overcome with curiosity about life on earth, made secret trips to the upper world. She always took the serpent's jewel with her because this great gem gave her power to come and go as she pleased. One day when she had risen to the surface she encountered a young man and an old woman. Frightened, she immediately returned to the water palace.

However, the young man, who was a prince, had caught a glimpse of her and had fallen in love with her. For hours he waited at the pond's edge, hoping that she would return. But when she did not, the young prince became deeply distressed.

After he had returned to his palace, he hardly ate any food. He refused to leave his room, vowing that he would never speak to anyone again until the lovely underwater creature became his bride. His father ordered the best doctors

Claude Monet: Nymphéas.

*...From their perch they saw that the pond was crowded
with brilliantly colored water lilies and with multicolored ferns...*

to the palace. But no matter how hard they tried, they were unable to cure the young prince. At last the king announced that he would offer half his kingdom and his beautiful daughter to anyone who could cure his son.

It came to pass that in the city there lived a poor but clever old woman, the mother of a strange son, Phakir Chand. When the old lady heard of the king's pronouncement, she was interested. She was very anxious for her son to marry the king's daughter. So, she went to the palace and asked for an audience with the king.

"Your Majesty," she said. "I believe I can cure your son of his peculiar illness."

The king looked at the woman in wonderment. For he could not understand how this frail old woman could succeed when the best doctors had failed.

"And do you know what is wrong with my son?" he asked.

"Indeed, I do," she answered with a smile.

"Then tell me what it is," the king said sternly.

"Your Majesty," the old woman replied, "if I reveal my secrets before I have treated your son, they will not work."

"All right, said the king. "Nothing will be lost by trying. When will you cure my son?"

"I can not give you any exact time, your Majesty. But I shall begin right away," the woman replied humbly.

"Is there anything you need?" asked the king.

"I should like a little shack to be built at the place where your son first became ill. I will also need some servants. And, finally, I have one favor to ask of you."

"And what is that?"

"I should like my son to gain the right to marry your daughter."

"My dear woman," answered the king, "if you succeed I shall gladly consent to your wish."

That very same day the woman moved into the shack near the edge of the pond.

Many weeks had passed since the princess had made her last trip to the surface of the pond. One day, while her husband was asleep, she took the jewel and rose upward. She looked around before going ashore, but seeing no one, she walked to the edge of the forest. As she started to comb her hair, the old woman quietly approached her and began speaking to her.

The princess was very much afraid at first. She soon relaxed when she realized that her visitor was just a kindly old woman.

"Why don't you let me hold the diamond?" asked the old woman. "It will make it easier for you to comb your hair."

The princess saw no harm in that and innocently handed the magic gem to the old lady.

But no sooner had she done that when the woman hid the diamond in her clothes, knowing that the princess was now in her power. Then she called the servants and they transported the crying princess into the city.

When the prince saw the beautiful water princess, he was cured immediately. He left his room and he dined with her.

Though he tried to persuade her to marry him immediately, she explained that she was married to the maharaja's son. The next two months were very sad for the lovely princess. She was very lonely for her husband. She made plots to escape, but realized that they could not possibly work because she needed the jewel in order to return to her water palace.

As the end of the year approached, elaborate plans were made for the wedding.

In the meantime, a year had passed since the son of the general had returned home and had explained what had happened to the maharaja's son. At the agreed upon day, the general's son had returned to the pond. He was waiting for his friend and the princess to rise to the surface. He waited for one, two, three days. But they did not come. Realizing that something must have happened, he started home.

His route led him through the city where the water princess was soon to be married. The town was gaily decorated with flags and banners. Musicians were parading through the streets. When he asked what the people were celebrating, he learned that a strange water princess was to marry their king's son. After having talked with many people, he understood all that had taken place. Then one old inhabitant told him about Phakir Chand.

"You know, the old woman is terribly worried, for her son, who is to marry the king's daughter, has not yet appeared. You probably know he's strange. He comes and goes, and no one ever knows when he's gone or when he's here."

"And what does he look like, this Phakir Chand?" asked the general's son.

"Oh, he's about your height, I'd say. But he doesn't wear any fancy clothes. He likes to rub his body with ashes. When he appears at his mother's house, he always dances a jig. Another thing that's strange about him is that he never says *yes*. If he wants to say yes, he says *hoom, hoom,* instead. He sure is funny," said the old man and shook his head.

"It's sort of strange that Phakir Chand of all people should marry the king's daughter," he continued. "But then again, no one knows the ways of this world. It must be written in the stars."

"I wouldn't be surprised," replied the general's son with a smile. "Things may not turn out as you might think."

For as the old man had talked, the general's son had formed a plan to rescue both the princess and his best friend.

"If I pretend to be Phakir Chand, I might be able to get into the old woman's house and find the jewel. And as Phakir Chand I should also be able to get into the palace."

He dressed himself to look like Phakir Chand. Then he rubbed his body with ashes and walked to the old woman's house. There he began to dance a jig. The old woman looked out the window and truly thought that it was her son who had returned.

"Well, it's a good thing that you're back," she said. "You must stay this time."

"I won't, I won't," replied the general's son.

"But you must," she said. "Besides wouldn't you like to see a jewel that's worth more than all the money in the king's treasury?"

"*Hoom, hoom,*" said the general's son. He entered the old woman's hut and she handed him the jewel. He immediately placed the diamond in his pocket.

"I will go to the king and tell him that you are here," said the woman. "Do you want to come along?"

"I won't, I won't. But tell him I'll go there later."

Thus when the general's son arrived at the palace looking like Phakir Chand, the guards let him enter without a question.

He entered the room where the water princess lived. At first she did not recognize him. When he identified himself, she was overjoyed to see her husband's best friend. Then she became very sad.

"If I do not escape by tomorrow morning, I shall be lost forever," she said. "For tomorrow evening is the day of the wedding."

"We shall try to escape, tonight," he said. "Just trust me, and be ready when I come for you."

As he left her room, he stopped and chatted with many of the guards. He wanted to make sure that they knew, that he—Phakir Chand—was in the palace, and that he had permission to come and go as he pleased.

He even danced his little jig from time to time, while shouting "*hoom, hoom.*"

Late that night he returned to the palace wearing an enormous cloak. When one of the guards questioned him about his outlandish costume, he merely smiled, said *"hoom, hoom, hoom,"* and danced his jig.

"I should have known better than to expect a logical answer from that crazy Phakir Chand," the guard said to himself. Then he continued his watch, pacing the long corridor.

A few seconds later, the general's son was in the princess' room.

"Quick," he commanded. "Hide under my cloak. We must get out of the palace before the guard returns."

The princess did as she was told. And within a minute or two they were outside the palace.

Immediately, they mounted two waiting horses and rode to the pond at a full gallop. There the general's son placed the magic jewel in the princess' hand. Then, hand in hand, they descended to the water palace below.

The king's son, who had been trapped in the palace for more than a year, was overjoyed to find that his wife and his best friend had finally returned. After much talk the three arose to the upper world and returned happily to their native land.

The real Phakir Chand returned home a few months after all the excitement. When his mother told him all that had taken place and how he had missed marrying the princess, he just smiled contentedly.

And then she asked: "Wouldn't you have liked to marry the princess?" He replied, "I wouldn't, I wouldn't."

And then, when she asked: "Are you happy now, my son?" He danced his jig and said *"hoom, hoom—hoom, hoom."*

The Field of Bauliauns

One holiday during harvest time, Tom Fitzpatrick was walking through the fields. As he passed a hedge, he heard some clacking and he stopped.

"It's strange," thought Tom, "to hear birds pecking and clacking away this late in the season."

Wondering where the noise was coming from, he peered over a wall that separated one field from another. But no sooner had he done that when the noise stopped. To his great surprise, however, he saw an earthenware jug filled to the brim with liquid. Next to it, sitting on a tree stump was a tiny man wearing a green cone-shaped hat. Tom watched with fascination as the little man dipped his cup into the jug and then drank it. All the time he was singing and humming to himself. Having drunk several cupfuls, he at last settled down and started to heel a shoe.

"If that isn't a sight to please any man," thought Tom to himself. "If I can just keep my eye on him, I can make a fortune. For the only way the leprechaun can escape me is if I look the other way."

Carefully he inched forward while staring at the little man. When he was standing next to him, Tom said:

"It's a nice day, neighbor. Why are you working today?"

"I work when I choose," the little man replied, not even looking at Tom.

"And what might you have, in that pitcher over there?" asked Tom.

"The best beer you can find in this part of the country."

"Beer?" shouted Tom in an astonished voice. "And where can you buy beer today?"

"You are a fool," replied the leprechaun. "I made it myself, of course. And you will never guess how I made it."

"With malt," Tom replied. "How else does one make beer?" Tom asked angrily.

"Well, you couldn't be more wrong," answered the leprechaun. "When the Danes came to Limerick they taught us how to make beer from heath. That's what I use. And I assure you, there's nothing like it."

"If it's that good, let me taste it," said Tom, who had developed an enormous thirst.

"Listen, lad," cackled the leprechaun. "You're wasting your time watching me. You'd be better off watching your sheep that are running wild all over your father's hay."

When Tom heard that, he was so surprised that he almost stopped looking at the little man to look into the pasture. Then he realized that if he had done that, the leprechaun would escape him. Furious that the leprechaun had nearly tricked him, he grabbed him by his shoulders and shook him as hard as he could.

"Come to your senses," shouted Tom. "Show me where your money is. Or I'll give you a thrashing you'll never forget."

When the leprechaun saw how very angry Tom was he became frightened.

"All right," he said. "My crock of gold is several fields away."

They set off and Tom held the leprechaun tightly and never took his eyes

*...They crossed hedges and ditches and walls
that enclosed fields...*

Vincent van Gogh: The Enclosed Field.

off him. They crossed hedges and ditches and walls that enclosed fields. It seemed to Tom that the little man was choosing the hardest way to go anywhere. But at last they came to a great field of boliauns.

There they stopped and the little man pointed to one of the flowers. "Dig beneath that boliaun," he said to Tom. "You'll find a crock of gold."

But Tom had nothing to dig with. He decided to run home to get a spade. But to make sure that he would find the boliaun again, he took off one of his garters and tied it to the flower.

"I've done my part," said the leprechaun. "I suppose you have no more need of me."

"You can go," replied Tom. "But you must promise that you will not take the garter from that boliaun."

"I will gladly promise you that," replied the little man with a wry smile on his face.

"Goodbye then, Tom," said the leprechaun. "And may the gold serve you well."

Tom ran home as fast as he could. He grabbed a spade and within an hour he was back at the field. But what he saw almost brought tears to his eyes. Thousands of boliauns had red garters exactly like his own tied to them. He would never find the gold now.

He returned home slowly with a heavy heart, cursing the wily leprechaun, who had tricked him so cleverly.

The Magic Walking Stick

In Bohemia many years ago, there lived a young pharmacist's apprentice who cared very much about his work. From early morning until late at night, Alfred Ritter prepared drugs that all the doctors ordered.

Whenever he had free time, he wandered into the fields and climbed mountains. He liked to collect unusual herbs, flowers, moss, and rocks. On rainy days Alfred stayed at home reading books and articles about foreign lands. For he had always wanted to visit the many marvels of the world.

Late one summer afternoon Alfred climbed a mountain to pick some flowers. The sun was just setting when on his way home, he met an old man who was bent under his load of brushwood.

"Let me help you," said Alfred. "The wood that you carry is much too heavy for you." And he took the wood from the old man and placed it on his back.

"That is very nice of you," said the old man. "But you better give it back to me for I have no money. I can not pay you anything for your labor."

"That's perfectly alright," replied Alfred. "I just want to help you out."

After edging their way up a narrow mountain path that seemed unfamiliar to Alfred, the old man asked Alfred what he had been doing in the mountains.

"I was collecting flowers and herbs," he replied. "But what I should like to do most of all is to travel. I would like to see the world's highest mountains as well as its great deserts. I should like to see large cities and beautiful oceans. But I know only too well that none of this will happen. I am just an apprentice in the village down in the valley. And one needs both money and time to travel."

"That's the difference between you and me," the old man said at last. "You are young and restless. You want to travel and see distant places. All I want is peace and quiet."

Finally they reached a broken-down shack. The old man pushed the door open and Alfred placed the firewood on the floor next to a pot-bellied stove. Then the old man took one of the sticks from the bundle and handed it to Alfred.

"Take this for your work," he said. "I wish I could give you something better, but I am afraid that it is all I have."

Alfred thanked the old man and left. He appreciated the idea that the old man had wanted to give him something. But he really didn't know what to do with this worthless stick. He didn't want to throw it away in case the old man was watching and would feel hurt. After he had walked for a few minutes, he realized he was no longer on the same path. In fact, nothing seemed familiar and he realized that he was lost. He retraced his steps but to his great surprise he could not even find the shack.

"How am I going to get back to town he thought. "I am sure there is a lot of work waiting for me, and I am going to be late."

"How I wish I were in the shop right now!" he said out aloud.

And when he looked up the forest had disappeared. He had mysteriously been whisked away and was standing in town.

How could that be?

One can not be in one place one second and in another the next. But he

Oskar Kokoschka: View of Stockholm Harbor.

. . . Standing in Stockholm harbor he watched
the fishing boats as they slowly wended their way toward the piers.
Dark clouds were hanging overhead . . .

knew that he was not dreaming. For in his hand he held the walking stick that the old man had given him.

As he looked at the stick and thought of the old man, he realized what had happened. The stick must be magic.

But to assure himself that this was true, he tested the cane again.

"I wish I were in Stockholm," he whispered.

He was there. Standing in the harbor he watched the fishing boats as they slowly wended their way to the piers. Dark clouds were hanging overhead. As much as Alfred wanted to remain there and look about, he knew that there was no time left and that he must return home.

"Please take me back to the pharmacy," he said. At the same moment he was back and at the door was the pharmacist warmly greeting his apprentice.

From that day on Alfred became the greatest traveler this world has ever known. One day he was on the top of Mount Everest, the next he was traveling across the Gobi desert on a camel. On the third day he was drifting on a raft down the rushing Colorado river in the Grand Canyon of the United States.

The years passed and one day the pharmacist called Alfred to his study and told him that he wanted him to take over the business. Alfred was pleased, of course, to find that so much trust had been placed in him. But above all he immediately realized that at last he would have more time to himself and that he would be able to spend a lot of time at all the places he had only seen briefly before.

When Alfred grew old and friends would visit him, they always wondered why Alfred always held an old, shabby stick of wood in his hands.

Radowid

In Bohemia, there once lived a farmer who was a great spendthrift. Though he owned much land and earned good money he was always in debt. One day, his creditors became so angry with him that they arrived at his home and demanded their money.

"I will pay you next month," he said to them. But they wanted the money right away and would not agree.

"Farmer," they replied, "we will give you twenty-four hours. If you do not have the money by then, we will take over your land."

Well, the farmer knew that he could do nothing. Certainly he could not raise the money in one day. Therefore, he asked his wife to pack their bags. On the very same evening, he, his wife, and his three daughters moved to an old deserted shack in the middle of a dense forest.

Since there was no food in the house, the farmer went hunting and shot a rabbit. Just as he was about to pick the animal up, an enormous bear appeared before him.

"Farmer," the huge animal growled in an angry voice, "you have no right to hunt on my land. I shall kill you unless you agree to give me your oldest daughter for my wife."

Since there was no escape and since the bear was so fierce, the farmer agreed to his terrible demand.

"In exactly two months I will come to fetch her," he roared and disappeared into the forest.

When the farmer returned to his shack he was so upset that his family knew something terrible must have happened. When he told them of his meeting with the bear, the oldest daughter said,

"Don't worry, Father. You did the right thing."

For seven weeks the farmer sat at home, holding his head in his hands, trying to think of a plan to save his daughter. During the eighth week he told his neighbors what had happened and asked them to bring arms to his house. If the bear arrived to claim the girl, they could try to scare him away. If that did not work, they would kill him.

On the fateful day, the neighbors were at his house, waiting for the beast. Evening came and the bear had not yet arrived. Then, as the last rays of the sun disappeared behind the horizon, a procession of golden carriages pulled by gray horses, drove up to the little shack. From the lead carriage leaped a handsome prince whose silk costume was embroidered with the finest gold filigree. He walked up to the farmer and asked to wed his eldest daughter.

"My good sir," said the farmer. "I am deeply honored, but unfortunately, I can not do as you ask. My oldest daughter is engaged to an enormous bear and we are waiting for him at this very moment."

"That is very bad," replied the prince. "For girls should wed men, and bears should wed bears."

"What you say is true," replied the father. "But what can I do?"

...In the lake many beautifully colored fish were swimming near the surface...

Emil Nolde: Fish.

"Do not worry, good farmer," replied the prince. "I will take care of everything."

The young prince talked so reassuringly that the farmer agreed. The wedding was held immediately. Although everybody was prepared to celebrate all night, the prince insisted that he would have to leave immediately. But before departing he presented a chest of gold pieces to his father-in-law.

Then, as mysteriously as the prince had arrived, he departed. It almost appeared to the farmer that the procession had not even reached the edge of the woods when it disappeared.

When the bear did not appear by midnight, the farmer knew that he and his family were safe. Grateful for this happy change of events, the farmer went to bed. And for the first time in eight weeks he enjoyed a good night's rest.

The next morning when the farmer opened the chest and saw all the glimmering gold pieces, he decided to give a big party. He had not learned his lesson and still believed that all his money could never be spent. So he went to town and bought many useless things. One morning he discovered that there were only a couple of gold pieces left. He was a poor man once again.

Off he went to the forest to hunt. It wasn't long before he had killed a wild goose. Just as he was about to pick the bird up, an eagle with a wider wing-spread than a man is tall, appeared before him.

"You have no right to hunt in my land," the eagle howled. "For this act, I will kill you unless you agree to give me your second daughter as my wife."

"I am sorry," said the farmer. "But I only killed the goose because my two daughters and my wife are hungry."

"It is too late to be sorry, farmer," the eagle screeched. He flew around the farmer and jabbed at him with his powerful talons.

"You give me no choice," said the farmer.

"I shall return for her in exactly two months," said the eagle.

Crying bitter tears, the farmer arrived at home. After having explained what had occurred, his second daughter said: "Don't be upset, Father. You did what you had to do."

On the last day of the eighth week, the farmer again asked his neighbors' help in fighting the eagle.

They waited all day, arms in hand, but the eagle did not appear. Just as the sun set, a group of horsemen blandishing swords came riding up to the shack. Behind them was a carriage drawn by eight black stallions. A young prince jumped from the carriage and approached the farmer.

"I should like to marry your second daughter," the handsome prince announced loudly.

"As much as I appreciate your offer, kind prince," the farmer replied, "I have already promised her to an eagle."

"No, farmer," said the prince. "You must not permit that. Girls should wed men, and birds should wed birds."

"What you say is true and I wish it were so," said the farmer. "But I can not go back on my word."

"I know what I am talking about," said the prince, "and I assure you that I shall take care of everything."

The farmer agreed to the prince's proposal. The wedding was celebrated immediately and within half an hour, the prince and his young bride rode away. Nobody could understand why they were in such a hurry. But the prince insisted that they had to leave. However, before he left he gave two chests of gold coins to his father-in-law.

When the eagle did not appear by midnight, the neighbors left, all very pleased by the happy events of that evening.

Now the farmer had two chests filled with gold coins. Most people would think that he would be more careful in spending his money. But nothing could be further from the truth. Within two months the new fortune was spent.

Once again he had to go into the forest to look for food. But instead of hunting, the farmer decided that it would be much safer to go fishing.

He cast his line in a deep lake where many beautifully colored fish were swimming. Within minutes he felt a tug on the line and he pulled a fish in. As he was unhooking his catch, a fish larger than a shark thrust its head through the surface of the water.

"Evil farmer," the large fish shrilled, "you shall pay with your life for having killed my friend, unless you promise to give me your youngest daughter for my wife."

The farmer gaped into the fish's mouth. It was lined with hundreds of sharp teeth.

"Make your decision," screamed the fish. "I have no time to lose."

The farmer once again felt that he had no choice and he promised his youngest daughter to the fish.

"I shall fetch her in exactly two months," he said.

Though the farmer and his wife were upset at the prospect of losing their last child, the daughter was not upset. She tried to comfort her father.

"You did what you had to do, dear Father," she said. "I am not afraid."

When the eight weeks had passed, the neighbors once again gathered at the farmer's house. They waited all day long, just as they had twice before, but the fish did not appear. And just at sunset the trampling of horses' hoofs could be heard in the distance. Soon, a carriage made of gold and diamonds drew up in front of the shack.

A handsome prince gracefully descended from it and walked over to the farmer.

"I should like to marry your youngest daughter," said he.

"I wish it were possible," answered the farmer. "But I have already promised her to an ugly fish."

"A fish should marry a fish; and a man should marry a woman," replied the prince. "Don't worry, I shall take care of everything."

The wedding was held immediately, and a few minutes later the prince announced that he and his bride would have to leave. No matter how hard the farmer tried to persuade the prince to stay, he would not listen. But before leaving he ordered that three chests of gold and jewels be given to his father-in-law.

With mixed emotions the farmer and his wife watched the couple disappear into the woods. They were pleased that their daughter had met a better fate than marrying a fish, but then too they were worried about their youngest child.

For their other two daughters had not sent them a word since their marriages. And now the youngest one had disappeared under similar mysterious circumstances.

The farmer was rich again and this time he was very careful. He bought some land and planted crops. Then he bought sheep, horses and cattle. Within a few years he was earning a fine living. Yet, most of the time, he and his wife were very sad. For they received no word from their daughters. It seemed as if they had vanished from the earth.

Three years after these strange events, the couple had a son, whom they called Radowid. Even though the farmer and his wife never talked about Radowid's three sisters, the lad sensed that there had been some tragedy in the family. One day, when he was sixteen years old, he noticed that his mother was crying.

"What is it, dear mother?" he asked gently. "Why do you cry? Why is it that both you and father are sad so very often?"

"Do not ask, my son," she replied.

But Radowid would not accept this answer. After much persuasion, his mother told him the story of his three sisters. Immediately Radowid decided to search for them.

His father tried to talk him out of this difficult task. But he soon realized that his son could not be dissuaded.

"Wish me well, dear parents," he said as he mounted his horse. "I promise that I shall return with my sisters."

After he had ridden for a few days, Radowid came to a large mountain. At first, he thought that he would ride around it. Then he noticed that smoke was rising near the top.

"I must climb the mountain and speak to whomever lives there. Perhaps they will know something about my sisters."

It was a long and difficult climb. At times he had to scale sheer cliffs. One false step and he would have fallen into the abyss hundreds of feet below. But he inched his way forward and after many hours he saw a cave. Inside it, a fire was burning and a lovely woman was playing with three small bears.

When she saw the strange lad enter the cave she became alarmed. "Who are you?" she gasped. "How did you get here?"

"I am looking for my sisters," replied Radowid "and perhaps you can help me find them."

Then he proceeded to tell her the strange story.

At once, the woman knew that the lad was her brother.

"I must hide you at once," she said. "There is not much time, for my husband will be back at any moment. And if he finds you, he will tear you to pieces."

And she hid her brother under her bed in the darkest corner of the cave. No sooner had she done that when a loud growl sounded throughout the cave and an enormous bear appeared.

"Wife," he said, "a human being is in this cave. Where is he?"

"That is impossible," she replied. "How could a human being climb this mountain?"

But the bear was not convinced. He looked all around the cave and finally came to the bed under which Radowid was hidden.

"There he is," the bear growled. He was about to drag Radowid out when the clock struck eight times. With the last stroke, the earth trembled and the cave turned into a magnificent chamber. The three bear cubs became three handsome young lads and the bear was transformed into the handsome prince who had come for the oldest sister many years earlier.

Immediately, the prince embraced his brother-in-law.

"We do not have much time, my friend," the prince said. "Let me explain to you the curse that was placed on me and my two brothers many years ago. Except for one hour a day when I am permitted to assume my real human shape, I must live as a bear. The same holds true for my brothers—one lives as an eagle and the other as a fish.

"I am not sure why we have all been cursed. It has something to do with my sister. How we may be freed of this dreadful curse I do not know either. But I suggest that you look for my brothers because they know more than I do."

Then the prince handed Radowid eight bear hairs. "Take these," he said. "If you should ever find yourself in a position where I might be able to help you, rub the hairs together and instantly eight bears will be there to help you."

"But now you must be on your way," he continued. "For when my hour is spent, I shall become a bear again and I shall have no control over what I do."

Radowid embraced his sister and thanked the prince.

"But how do I find your brothers?" he asked.

"I do not know the way," replied the prince. "But outside this room you will find a carriage waiting for you. The horses know the way."

Radowid seated himself in the carriage and immediately the carriage started to move so rapidly that the young lad thought he was flying.

Just as the magic hour was over, Radowid reached the border of the bear's kingdom. They had reached an invisible line over which the carriage could not cross. As Radowid got out of the carriage and walked on, he felt the earth tremble. He turned around and saw the carriage and horses disappear.

He walked for many hours. As he neared a forest, he noticed that one of the trees towered above all others. Looking up he saw a tree house near the top branches. He was certain that this must be the home of the sister who was married to the eagle. He climbed the tree and when he reached the house he knocked on the door.

"Who is it?" a woman asked in a gentle voice.

"Your brother," replied Radowid.

"Brother? You must be mistaken!"

"Indeed not," said Radowid. "Open the door."

The woman let him in. Radowid explained to her all that had taken place. Soon she realized that Radowid really was her brother, that he had told her the truth.

"My husband will be here any minute. You must hide, otherwise he will try to kill you," the lovely girl said to Radowid.

And as she was talking, the tree began to sway and a huge eagle settled on one of the branches.

No sooner had Radowid hidden himself under her bed when the eagle entered.

"There is something wrong," he screeched. "It seems to me that a man is here."

"Now aren't you silly, said the girl. "How could a man come here?"

As he began searching for Radowid, the clock struck nine. On the last stroke, the hut turned into a castle, and the eagle into a handsome prince.

"I can not tell you more than my older brother has," he said to Radowid as he embraced him. "But you must find my youngest brother. I think he will know more. Take the carriage that is waiting for you below. It will lead you to a distant country. When the carriage reaches the end of my kingdom, follow the rocky road that will be in front of you. The road will lead you to a pond. At the exact moment when a wild goose flies overhead, dive into the water. But before you leave, take these eight eagle feathers with you. Should you ever be in trouble, rub them together and eight eagles will be at your side, ready to help you. Now hurry, my dear brother-in-law. Soon I shall lose my human shape. Then I shall have no control over my actions."

Radowid left his sister and got into the carriage. Within minutes, they reached the magic border that his brother-in-law had talked about. He jumped down from the carriage and followed the rocky road that led him to a pond. He had not been there long when he noticed the wild goose flying overhead. Instantly he plunged into the water.

As he swam underwater, he heard a clock strike ten. At the last stroke the pond was transformed into a magnificent castle. Standing at the gate were his sister and his brother-in-law. But this time no explanations were needed. They seemed to be expecting him.

"My dear Radowid," the prince said in a gentle and sad voice. "Are you certain that you want to try to free us from our curse? For let me warn you immediately that it is a most difficult undertaking."

"I am not afraid," said Radowid. "I have sworn that I would not return home without my sisters."

"Well then, there is a chance that you will succeed. But first let me tell you about our enchantment. A very long time ago an evil wizard wanted to marry our sister. When she refused, he transformed us into a bear, an eagle, and a fish. Then he took our sister to his underground cave and vowed that we could not live as human beings until she agreed to marry him. Since she has refused to do this, we are still cursed."

"But is there no way to free you?" asked Radowid.

"There is," replied the youngest brother, "but it is very difficult and very dangerous."

"First of all you must enter his cave. But to do that you must find a key made of diamonds that is placed in the hollow of a tree nearby. Once you have this key you must walk through five strange rooms. In the sixth room you will find our sister lying on a bed of solid gold. But she will not be alone, for the wizard guards her day and night. Above her bed you will see a golden hunting horn. You must take this horn and blow three blasts on it. On the third blast, the curse will be lifted from all of us, and the wizard will lose all his power."

"Nothing can stop me," said Radowid. "I shall leave immediately."

He bade farewell to his sister and brother-in-law. He walked all night long. And though he could not see in the darkness, he knew that he was on the right path. He felt as if some invisible force were directing him.

The next morning he found himself before a cave whose entrance was closed by a heavy granite door. On the side of the cave he saw a tall cypress tree with a hole in it. He climbed the tree and saw the key. But just as he was going to take it, the tree began to move. Looking down he saw that several bulls were trying to unearth the tree. Quickly he took the eight bear hairs and rubbed them together. Eight bears appeared instantly and chased the bulls away.

Once again he tried to seize the key. But just before he reached it a strange bird appeared and flew off with the ring in its beak. He rubbed the eagle's feathers together. Instantly eight eagles were in the sky. They overtook the strange bird, retrieved the ring and dropped it into Radowid's outstretched hand.

Quickly Radowid climbed down the tree. Carefully, he examined the granite door. But he could not find the keyhole. In despair he tapped the massive door with the key and quite unexpectedly the door flew open.

He entered the cave and soon stumbled into the first room. It was a chamber of fire. Flames soared to the ceiling and the heat was unbearable. He could smell his hair burning. With an extra effort he fled to the second room. This was a room of ice and so cold that his feet began to freeze to the ground. He forced himself through this room only to enter one that was filled with poisonous snakes and lizards. Horrified, he jumped over them and entered the fourth room. There he found scorpions and bats, tarantulas and owls. Quickly he ran on. In the fifth room he saw shapeless monsters—some with almost human faces—crawling and floating toward him.

In absolute terror, he somehow managed to pass these horrible creatures.

The sixth room was exactly as his brother-in-law had described. Lying on a bed made of solid gold was the loveliest girl Radowid had ever seen. Seated in the corner, asleep, was the evil wizard. Above the girl's bed Radowid saw the hunting horn. As he silently crept toward the horn, a clock struck twenty times. At the last chime, the wizard asked:

"And now, my pretty one, will you become my wife?"

"Never!" replied the girl without opening her eyes.

"Then your brothers will be condemned forever; and you will sleep here for all time!"

Radowid seized the horn, placed it to his lips and gave a loud blast. The wizard jumped up. But before he could reach Radowid, he had already sounded a second blast. Then came a third clear blast and a huge explosion.

Instantly the wizard disappeared into thin air.

At the same time the princess awoke from her sleep. When she and Radowid looked at each other, they fell deeply in love.

They left the cave for the castle of the youngest brother. When they arrived all the brothers were waiting. That same day all six of them set out for the home of Radowid's parents.

The wedding celebrations for Radowid and his lovely bride lasted for an entire month. Everyone from near and far was invited to the feasts.

Eventually the three princes and Radowid wisely ruled over a vast land and over a very happy and contented people.

Honoré Daumier: Riot Scene.

*...He saw shapeless monsters—some with almost human
faces—that crawled and floated toward him...*

About the Great Painters...

Jean Baptiste Camille Corot 1796–1875. French landscape painter. Born in Paris. Under the tutelage of classical painters Michallon and Bertin, Corot began his art studies at the age of 26. After various trips to Italy (1825, 1834, 1843), Corot became a frequent winner at the Paris Salon, and was often appointed to its jury. His paintings of this early period—including *Coliseum* and *Forum* (both in the Louvre)—are notable for their clear lighting and delicate compositional balance. He is known primarily for his later landscapes, painted in varying shades of gray and green, and always reflecting his lyrical temperament and his sensitive use of lighting. A leading member of the Barbizon School, Corot also painted such excellent portrait and figure studies as *Femme à la Perle* (Louvre) and *Interrupted Reading* (Art Institute, Chicago). Among his several hundred landscapes are *Une Matinée* (1850, Louvre), *La Lac* (1861), *L'Arbre Brisé* (1865), and *Pastorale—Souvenir d'Italie* (1873). An extremely gentle man, his kindly interest in people earned him the nickname "Papa Corot."

Lucas Cranach 1472–1553. German painter and engraver. (His last name is also spelled Kranach). He was known as the *elder* to distinguish him from his son Lucas, the *younger*. The real family name was either Müller or Sunder. Lucas settled in Wittenberg in 1504, and was made court painter under three electors of Saxony. Lucas kept a successful workshop in the town and was twice elected burgomaster. He was a friend of Martin Luther, and supported the Lutheran teachings, in numerous pictures and woodcuts. For this he has often been called the Reformation painter. He was a fast and prolific painter, the reason, perhaps, why his work is uneven in quality. His portraits were highly successful. Among his best-known works are *Repose in Egypt, Crucifixion, Unknown Female,* and *Self-Portrait.* He also designed some impressive woodcuts and copperplates.

Honoré Daumier 1808–1879. French painter and caricaturist. After earning his living doing illustrations for music publishers and advertisements, Daumier joined the staff of the Parisian comic journal *Caricature,* where he began his career of creating scathing cartoons directed against the bourgeoisie and the government. A barbed cartoon which portrayed Louis Philippe as Gargantua earned Daumier a six-month prison term in 1832. But upon his release he joined another political magazine *Charivari,* for which he worked until 1864. For this journal Daumier produced nearly 4,000 lithographs, which portrayed social hypocrisy and corruption in a bitterly realistic style. These works, enjoyed in their day as popular political satire, are now considered masterpieces both for their penetrating wit and their amazingly original execution. One of the great forerunners of the naturalist movement, Daumier also executed about 200 canvases marked by his characteristic dramatic intensity and clarity of vision. Among these works are *Christ and His Disciples* (Rijks Museum, Amsterdam), *Republic* (Louvre), *Three Lawyers* (Philipps Gallery, Washington, D.C.) and *Don Quixote* and *The Third-Class Carriage* (both Metropolitan Museum). A skillful sculptor, Daumier's work can be seen in the Walters' Art Gallery, Baltimore.

Eugène Delacroix 1798–1863. French painter, he was born near Paris. He studied at the École des Beaux Arts under Guérin. He achieved distinction as leader of the Romantic School of French art. He was often at variance with the official pronouncements of the Academicians on paintings. One of his earliest works, *Dante and Virgil* (1822), brought him fame. Always a controversial figure, such influential admirers as Thiers and Baudelaire assured him some respect as well as commissions. After a trip to Morocco in 1832, he painted a number of canvases, notably *Women of Algiers.* He painted murals for the Hôtel de Ville in Paris, the Libraries of the Luxembourg and the Louvre's Gallery of Apollo. He was author of the *Journals of Eugène Delacroix,* a brilliant work which mirrors the problems of the artist of the day, and society's standards, prejudices, and beliefs. Dynamic composition and color distinguished his works, which are represented in many of the world's museums.

Thomas Gainsborough 1727–1788. English landscape and portrait painter. Born in Sudbury, ninth son of a cloth merchant. In 1740, when he was thirteen, Gainsborough became the assistant and pupil of Hubert Gravelot, the French engraver, who lived in London. During his formative period Gainsborough also studied the landscapes of Ruisdael and Wynants, the 17th century Dutch artists, and was much influenced by the work of Francis Hayman. Five years later he returned to Sudbury, and at the age of eighteen married Margaret Burr. His wife's income of two hundred pounds a year, and her stable temperament were decisive factors in starting him off in his career. In these early years as a painter he loved to draw and paint the countryside around Sudbury and Ipswich, often using them as backgrounds for his portraits. The landscape of these pictures is always young and fresh, full of the shimmer and open-air feeling that later made him famous. In 1759 Gainsborough went to Bath, the fashionable spa of 18th century England, and soon obtained commissions for portraits of aristocrats. Later he moved to London, where his circle of admirers grew, commissions poured in, and he became the only real rival of Sir Joshua Reynolds, then the fashionable portrait painter of the day. Gainsborough is famous for the elegance in his portraits, and his paintings of women in particular have great delicacy and refinement, learned partially from Van Dyck. As a colorist Gainsborough is unrivaled among English painters. His greatest paintings are full of quivering life, a light, airy quality, with greens and blues predominating. Unlike Sir Joshua, Gainsborough had little time for the members of high society; he preferred to spend his time painting landscapes, which at the time he could not sell. These have since been recognized as the first great English landscapes, and have rarely been surpassed. Unlike most portrait painters of that period, Gainsborough is believed to have painted all parts of his pictures himself. Among the best known of his works are *The Blue Boy* (Huntington Art Gallery, San Marino), *Lady Innes* and *The Mall* (both Frick Collection, New York), and *Perdita Robinson* (Wallace Collection, London). There are other Gainsboroughs in the national galleries in England, Ireland, and Scotland, as well as in the Metropolitan Museum, New York, and museums in Boston, Cincinnati, Philadelphia, and St. Louis.

Ando Hiroshige 1797–1858. Japanese landscape painter and color-woodcut artist. His soft, mystical way of handling such subject matter as snow scenes, moonlight scenes, rain and mist deeply impressed Whistler and a number of the impressionist painters. His prints can be seen in the principal museums of the world, including the Louvre in Paris, the Metropolitan Museum of Art in New York, and the National Gallery in London.

Eitoku Kano 1543–1590. One of the most prolific and original painters of the Kano school. He painted landscapes and figures on screens. He used gold paints frequently, thereby endowing his work with a lavishness and splendor that was heretofore unknown in Japan. Also unlike other Japanese painters of his era, as well as painters of the Kano school, his style was looser, less precise and more free. Much of his time was spent decorating the interiors of the royal palaces. A fine example of his work, *Pines on Snow Mountains* can be seen at the Freer Gallery of Art, Washington, D.C.

Oskar Kokoschka 1886–   . Born in Bohemia. He entered the Vienna School of Arts and Crafts in 1905. In 1908 he was expelled from the school for his expressionist drawings and plays which had shocked the public. Between 1908 and 1914 he worked as an illustrator for the magazine *Der Sturm.* During that period he also painted a series of portraits of actors and writers. Unlike the so-called realistic classical portraits, these works are endowed with profound psychological interpretation of character. In 1916, Kokoschka was badly wounded in battle, and it took many years for him to regain his health. Between 1924 and 1931 he lived in Dresden but traveled extensively throughout Europe and North Africa. With the rise of National Socialism in Germany, Kokoschka's work along with those of other expressionist painters was declared decadent and removed from the museums. In 1934 he fled to Prague. In 1937 he issued an important statement attacking the Nazi and fascist political structure. And, as a final gesture of defiance he painted a pure, expressionist self-portrait entitled, "Portrait of a Degenerate Artist." Among his most important works are portraits of Ambassador Maisky (Tate Gallery) London, the double-portrait of Hans and Erica Tietze-Conrat (Museum of Modern Art) and many landscapes. He also wrote several verse dramas.

Claude Monet 1840–1926. French impressionist painter, he was born in Paris. He became the leading painter of the Impressionist movement; indeed it was his *Impression-Sunrise,* first exhibited in 1874, which gave the movement its name. Soon after his birth, his family moved to Le Havre and he first studied art there, under Boudier. In 1862 he returned to Paris, and there he met Renoir, Cézanne, and Sisley. He and Sisley organized the Exhibition of 1874. For a long time his style remained unpopular, and he lived in poverty, but in 1883, a near-successful exhibition enabled him to buy a property at Giverny near Vernon, where he spent the remainder of his life painting. He painted many scenes several times, but always in a different light, because he and the impressionists saw color as the result of reflections from surrounding objects. Waterloo Bridge and Rouen Cathedral, for instance, appear in the blue of dawn, the glare of noonday light, the blood red of sunset, and the gray of dusk. For the last ten years of his life he was almost blind. His work is represented in the Art Institute of Chicago and the Metropolitan Museum of Art in New York.

Emil Nolde 1867–1956. German expressionist painter. After teaching for six years (1892-1898) he devoted all his time to painting. He was one of the members of the new German expressionist group of painters who called themselves, *Die Brucke*—meaning, "The Bridge." This movement intended to bridge the "old" art with the "new" art. He was a superb colorist. The range of his subject matter was broad. He painted from nature—seascapes, flowers—as well as strictly from his imagination. Although his work was removed from German museums during the Nazi period because of the "decadence" they claimed was inherent in all expressionistic work, Nolde today ranks as one of Germany's finest 20th century painters. His works can be found in many German museums, as well as in the great art museums throughout the world.

Harmenszoon van Rijn Rembrandt 1606–1669.
Dutch painter and etcher. He was born in Leiden and, at the age of 12, became apprenticed to Van Swanenburgh, there. After two years he moved to Amsterdam for further study under Pieter Lastman. In 1623 he returned to his home town of Leiden and remained there for the next eight years. Here he painted his earliest pictures e.g. *Paul in Prison,* and *St. Jerome.* In 1631, he returned to Amsterdam and settled there. Here he did most of his outstanding work. In 1634, he married Saskia van Ulyenburgh, who was the model for many of his best paintings. In 1656, he was declared bankrupt, and a collection of his drawings and etchings was sold for 500 florins, a mere fraction of their real value. Rembrandt continued to work hard and in the closing years of his life produced some of his best works. He was one of the world's greatest painters of all time. His most important works include *Presentation in the Temple* (1631), *Lesson in Anatomy* (1632), *Descent from the Cross* (1633), *Saskia* (1638), *The Night Watch* (1642), *The Polish Rider* (1658), and *The Jewish Bride* (1663). During his lifetime he painted some fifty self-portraits.

Joseph Mallord William Turner 1775–1851.
British landscape artist. He was born in London, son of a barber. Turner had little formal education. In 1789, he entered the Royal Academy School. A few years later he exhibited his first oil paintings. He was made an associate member of the Academy in 1799 and a full academician in 1803. Turner's early style reflected the influence of the Dutch landscape masters, as seen in his *Sun Rising Through Vapors* (National Gallery, London). From 1880 on, he earned sufficient money to permit him to travel widely through Europe, where he made thousands of drawings which were the basis for many of his great oil paintings. First painting in the classical manner, frequently after the style of Claude Lorrain, he later developed his own individualism. He was bitterly attacked by the critics, being considered by them to be too abstract; but he was brilliantly defended by John Ruskin. Turner willed all his works to the British people, and all are in British museums, including *The Calais Pier, Sun Rising in the Mist, Snow Storm,* and *The Whale Ship.*

Vincent Van Gogh 1853–1890. Dutch post-impressionist painter. Born in Holland. The son of a clergyman. Van Gogh had a variety of jobs before becoming a painter at the age of twenty-seven. This was only ten years before his tragic suicide, and it is a great loss to art that he did not take up his brush sooner. As a young man he worked for a picture dealer and then turned to evangelism. He began to preach to the miners, but was quickly dismissed for over-zealousness. In 1880 he began to paint. His early work, executed between 1880 and 1885, is known as his Dutch Period.

The pictures he painted at this time reflected his locale, life among the miners, and his own miserable existence. The canvases were dark and brooding, the most famous of them, exemplifying his early style, being *The Potato Eaters.* The five years he painted in Holland were full of hardships. Extreme poverty and several broken romances drove him to the brink of despair. In 1886, his devoted younger brother Theo rescued him. Theo Van Gogh had always tried to give Vincent moral and financial support, and he brought the artist to live with him in Paris. Here Van Gogh met such painters as Degas, Pissarro, Gauguin, Seurat, and Signac. Gauguin became his friend; Seurat and Signac influenced his work. Impressed by these two neo-impressionists, he adopted their more scientific and precise approach known as pointillism, and the brighter palette they advocated. This period lasted only briefly. In 1888, ravaged by ill health, he took a house in Arles, in South Eastern France, and persuaded Gauguin to join him. At this time Van Gogh had his first attack of insanity, when he cut off his ear. He was confined to Arles Hospital, then to the asylum at Saint-Remy. In spite of his illness he continued to paint, almost feverishly. During the last two years of his life he had long intervals of lucidity, and his paintings of this period show a rare and extraordinary beauty and great intensity. He expressed the frenzy and intensity of his unique vision in violent color contrasts, most notably in the magnificent landscapes, portraits, and still lifes of this last period. These paintings were to be his final and unrivaled legacy to the world, among them such pictures as *L'Arlesiènne* (Metropolitan Museum), *Le Café de Nuit, The Sunflowers* (Louvre), *The Starry Night* (Museum of Modern Art, New York). In 1890, Van Gogh despaired of ever being cured and shot himself. He was 37 years old.

Adriaen van Ostade 1610–1684. He was born in Haarlem, Holland, the son of a poor weaver. In 1627 he was an apprentice of the master painter Frans Hals. By the time he was 24 years old he had already attained sufficient skill as an artist to be accepted to the Haarlem Guild. From 1646 to 1661 he was a member of the board of directors of the Guild and in 1662 he became its dean. He is most famous for his paintings of typical village scenes and peasant life. Haarlem is a suburb of Amsterdam and Van Ostade was able to meet Rembrandt. The influence of this master's work can be seen in Van Ostade's paintings produced between 1650 and 1660. Among his most famous works are: *The Drinker* (Louvre), *The Old Fiddler* (Metropolitan Museum). Aside from painting in oils, Ostade produced numerous watercolors, drawings, and fine copper engravings.